KITMAN AND WILLY AT SEA

Best Wishes
Chris Demarest

BY CHRIS L. DEMAREST

SIMON & SCHUSTER BOOKS FOR YOUNG READERS
Published by Simon & Schuster
New York · London · Toronto · Sydney · Tokyo · Singapore

SIMON & SCHUSTER BOOKS FOR YOUNG READERS
Simon & Schuster Building, Rockefeller Center,
1230 Avenue of the Americas, New York, New York 10020

Copyright © 1991 by Chris L. Demarest

SIMON & SCHUSTER BOOKS FOR YOUNG READERS
is a trademark of Simon & Schuster
The text of this book is set in 16 pt. Stempel Schneidler.
The display type was hand-lettered by Anthony Bloch.
The illustrations are watercolor and ink.
Designed by Vicki Kalajian
Manufactured in the United States of America

10   9   8   7   6   5   4   3   2   1

Library of Congress Cataloging-in-Publication Data
Demarest, Chris L. Kitman & Willy at sea. Summary: Kitman and Willy
find themselves on a remote island where a sinister someone
is trapping all the animals, until Kitman and Willy beat
him at his own game. [1. Cats—Fiction. 2. Mice—Fiction.
3. Trapping—Fiction. 4. Islands—Fiction.] I. Title.
II. Title: Kitman and Willy at sea. PZ7.D3914Ki 1991 [E]—dc20 90-46837
ISBN 0-671-65696-1

For Simon

"It's too hot to work today," thought Kitman and Willy.
"We should do something that's fun."

"We should go on a voyage," Willy said, racing off.
"Yes," answered Kitman, "a long one."

In a flash they headed for the dock.
"This will be great," called Willy.

With a heave-ho, Kitman readied the boat.

"Full speed ahead," called Willy.
"Aye, aye," said Kitman as the wind filled
their boat's sail.

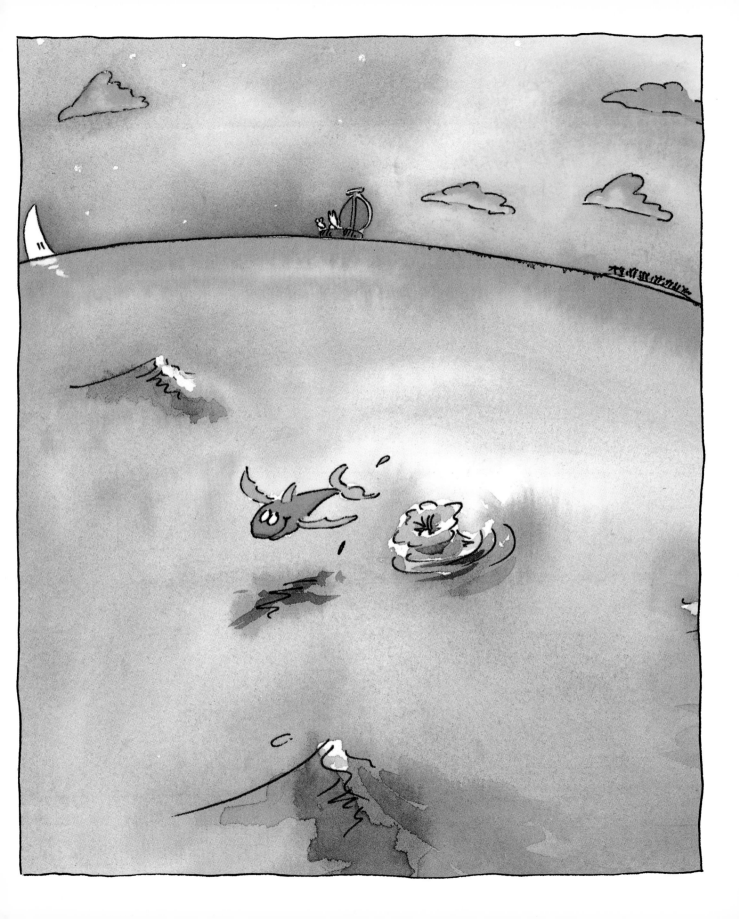

As their boat drifted toward an island,
Kitman and Willy prepared to go ashore.

"Iron away," yelled Willy, aiming for a giant rock.

But it was no rock.
"Ouch!" cried out an elephant.

"Are you with the man?" he whimpered.
Kitman and Willy shook their heads.

"A horrible man is catching all my friends," explained the elephant, "and soon he'll find me."

"This is terrible," whispered Willy.
"We must do something. But what?"

They thought very hard.
"I know," said Kitman. "Let's make an animal
he'll be sure to want."

Clop! Clop! Clop! The strange creature paraded through the jungle, leaving the most unusual footprints and making a terrible noise.

Left, right, the man listened.
Then he spotted the tracks.

"Now," said Kitman.
"It's time to lay the trap."

While the man stalked the strange beast,
Kitman, Willy, and the elephant went to work.

Closer and closer the man crept.

Then he saw it.

"CHARGE!" he cried out.

"Hooray," yelled the elephant.
"We did it," cheered Kitman and Willy.

"Now for a taste of his own medicine," said the elephant.

"There's only one thing left to do,"
said Kitman and Willy.

Everyone paraded down to the shore...

and waved good-bye to Kitman and Willy.